Silent Eclipse
When Darkness hides the truth
Pooja Rajnani

The Pooja & Tania Press

For Tania.

My inspiration.

My dedication.

My reason to keep going.

Thank you for always believing in me and loving me.

P.S. I am so proud of you —

for the beautiful and kind young woman you are growing up to be.

“Nothing is ever really lost to us as long as we remember it.”

— L.M. Montgomery

Trigger Warning

This novel contains themes of psychological trauma, emotional manipulation, death, and disturbing supernatural events. Reader discretion is advised.

If you are sensitive to content involving familial abuse, possession, or mental instability, please proceed with caution.

Prologue

The dream always starts the same.
A chapel.
No roof.
Just stars — or maybe holes in the sky.

I'm wearing red.
Not fabric.

Blood.

I'm standing in the center, barefoot, something cold around my neck.
The clock behind me ticks louder than my thoughts.
3:12.

A voice says: *"She must choose."*

I turn.

Three shadows wait at the altar.
One holds a blade.
One holds a ring.
One... wears my name.

I open my mouth to speak —
but I don't remember which one I am.

I wake up, gasping.
The clock by my bed reads **3:12.**

Chapter 1

In the last days of who we used to be.

"Zara, do you think we'll ever be able to run away from this hell of a place we call home?"

Zara Kapoor — my best friend since before she was even born.
My sister.
I always tease her, saying she was our parents' mistake, born nine years after me.
She's the only friend I have.
Maybe the only friend I'll ever have.

"Come on, didi, you know this isn't the time to talk about it. Mum's around. If she hears you say that, you know what'll happen."

"I just know I can't live here anymore. The way Mum and Baba treat us — does that seem normal to you? I hate being at home. They don't even let us go anywhere!"

My mother, Leela Kapoor, is a well-known psychologist.
She's seen more darkness than any of us.

And I despise that she sees everything — but still chooses silence.
Sometimes I want to slap her awake.

She unravels everyone's mind but her own.
With hers, she runs. From the truth. From us.

Maybe Baba was never evil. Just a man who didn't deserve daughters like us — or a wife who shielded his truth while burning in it.

"Zara! Mira! Come to the living room. Now!"

The command cracked through the house like thunder.

Zara grabbed my hand before I could move — her fingers trembling, nails
digging into my palm.
She knew what was coming.
And suddenly... so did I.

We stood in front of our mother — jaw clenched, fists curled, as if she needed
to hit something just to feel in control again.

"You've been sneaking around the basement again?" she hissed, eyes locked on
Zara.
"Going through old boxes? Reading things you had no business touching?"

Zara shook her head — but it was too late.
I could see the truth written all over her face.
She knew.
And now, so did I.

The belt lifted before I could speak.
The whistle through the air was the only warning.

Smack.

I hit the floor hard.
Pain bloomed in my ribs. Blood pooled in my mouth.
But it was nothing compared to what was rising in my chest.

Mum froze.
Her face twisted — not in guilt, but panic.

Because now, I knew.

"You're afraid of the truth," I whispered.

She didn't answer.

I pushed myself up and turned to Zara — her face streaked with tears, her eyes
full of a shame that was never hers to carry.

"Go pack your bag," I said softly. "Don't ask questions."

She hesitated.
But something in my voice made her move.

Then I looked back —

At the woman who raised us.
The woman who let truth rot in the walls of this house believing it would never find us.

"You always stood there watching; you did this to us. I hope it was worth it, because now you have to watch us leave and you can't do anything."

She gasped. Tears welled.
But I'd had enough of performances.

"We're not your daughters anymore.
We're just the ghosts you tried to silence."

And I walked away.
From the past.
From the lies.
From the house where monsters weren't under the bed —
they were invited in.

Chapter 2

When you walk away from a place that once defined your existence, everything fractures.
It doesn't matter how broken it was — it was *yours*.
And when you leave, you don't heal.

You adapt.

You learn to move around the ruins inside you like furniture in a burning house.

It's December 3rd.
Five days since we left.
Five days without sleep.
Five days of empty stomachs and heavier hearts.

I think I'm starting to hallucinate.
Earlier, I saw Zara talking to someone. Alone. Laughing softly… and then crying.
And there were marks on her arms I hadn't noticed before.
Thin. Sharp. Almost deliberate.

They had to be illusions, right?

But the shadows under her eyes aren't illusions.
They're deep. Hollow. Like something inside her is caving in.
She looks ready to collapse, a dam straining against its own weight.
Still. Quiet.

But if she breaks, it won't be with a whimper.
It'll be a flood.

We're headed somewhere we were forbidden to ever speak of — let alone return to.
The place where our grandparents died.
The manor.

I know it's dangerous.
But it's our last option.

We're somewhere near the south of Birmingham now.
Still too far to feel safe.
Too close to keep pretending I have a plan.

I reach for Zara's hand.

She isn't there.

I whip around — and my breath leaves me.
She's collapsed on the ground.
Unmoving.

Panic claws through my chest as I rush to her side.
Her skin is pale.
Her cheek, when I touch it, is ice.

I feel the regret rise like bile.
This is all my fault.

No food. No rest.
No roof over our heads.

I dragged her into this — chasing freedom like it wouldn't come with a price.

I ease her head onto my lap, trying to elevate her slightly.
Unscrew the cap of the water bottle with shaking hands.
Pour a little into her mouth.

She stirs.
And then — she opens her eyes slowly.

She sees me.
And for the first time in five days, she really *sees* me.

She throws her arms around me and breaks down.
She cries like she's been holding it in since the day we were born.

"Mira... what have we done?" she sobs.
"We left home. Where will we go? What's going to happen to us?"

Her voice cracks — anger and fear tangled like thorns in her throat.

"You doomed us, Mira! We're homeless. Broke.
I was *surviving* in that house — but you took away the only shelter we had!"

She blames me.
Over and over.
And I let her.

Because if she's yelling, she's breathing.
If she's crying, she's still mine.

I sit there like a corpse with its eyes wide open, letting every word bruise me.
As long as she holds on — I can take it.

She doesn't know what I know.
Doesn't see what I saw.

She doesn't remember the way she started forgetting things.
The way she'd drift off mid-sentence.
Forget names. Faces.
I'd call her, and she'd blink at me like I was a stranger.

Leela and Baba were breaking her.
Slowly. Systematically.
Twisting her mind until she didn't know who she was unless they told her.

That house was killing her.

And I couldn't just sit back and let them erase the only person who ever loved
me without condition.

So no — I don't regret running.
Even if it means sleeping on the streets.
Even if she hates me right now.

Because if I hadn't taken her away...

She wouldn't be crying in my arms.
She wouldn't be alive.

Chapter 3

We survived one more night.

The key in my pocket feels warm against my palm.
Heavier than it was six days ago.
Maybe it's the weight of everything we've run from —
or everything we're walking toward.

Either way, I can't let go of it.
The next choice I make might change everything.
But it's the only one that might save us.

We have to go to Kohl Manor.
It's not a matter of courage anymore.
It's survival.

Zara's hand grips mine — tight, desperate; as if letting go for even a second would make me vanish forever.

I look down at her.
Eighteen next month.
And already, she's seen her whole world collapse like a house of glass.

I want to promise her that things will get better.
But all I can promise is that I'll fight to keep her breathing.

This isn't how our story ends.
And if it is...

Then let it end screaming; not silently.

—

Hours pass.
Walking. Hiding.
Avoiding people. Avoiding eyes.

Finally, we reach the edge of a dense, overgrown forest.

Zara hesitates.
"Mira... this doesn't look safe. What if something happens? Please. Let's go back. It's not too late."

Her voice wavers like a child's, lost in the wrong world.

I don't have the luxury of fear — not out loud.

"Zara... I know you're scared. So am I. But we can't turn back."

I face her fully.
"That house we left... that wasn't our home. It never was.
We've come too far to undo it all now.
If we go back, we lose everything.
Trust me. Please — just this once."

She stares at me — eyes wide with dread.
And nods.
Barely.

We step into the forest.

The air shifts.
Colder. Quieter.

Even the birds have gone silent.

Each branch creaks beneath our feet like a warning.
The deeper we go, the denser it becomes.

The trees seem to bend inward — listening.

Our hands remain locked.
Heartbeats thumping in unison.
Waiting for something — anything — to leap out at us.

I can't let her see me hesitate.
But I do.
I always do — quietly, where she can't reach.

Then I see it.

A faint blue glow surrounds us.
Like mist.
Like something watching.

I hear Zara gasp.
She sees it too.

The temperature drops so fast I can see our breath fogging up in front of us.

I take off my jacket and wrap it around her shoulders.

As I do, a new light appears ahead.
Golden. Flickering.
Like a pathway.

It wasn't there a second ago.

Is it a coincidence or is it my hallucinations again?

I don't know.
I just know I'm running out of lies — even the comforting ones.

—

We reach the entrance of Kohl Manor.

No guards.
No danger.
Just silence.

The iron gates are tangled in thick vines and thorns — grown wild over years of abandonment.

But the moment I take the key out of my pocket —

The vines recoil.

Not break. Not fall.
Recoil.

They hiss as they pull back, like metal striking water.

As if the key frightened them.

I freeze.

But then I turn to Zara — and she's staring too.
She saw it.

She looks at me, eyes wide with something beyond fear.

I try to stay calm.
But it feels like swallowing broken glass.

We move forward in silence.

The mansion looms ahead — massive, ancient.
It looks more like a universe than a house.

The land around it stretches endlessly, wrapped in mist, refusing to give away
any secrets.

We reach the main door.

I slide the key into the lock — but it won't twist.

My palms sweat.
I try again.
And again.
Nothing.

Zara touches my shoulder. "Let me try."

She places her fingers on the key —

And it glows.

Like it belongs to her.
Like it was waiting for her.

The lock clicks.
The door creaks open.

And for the first time in my life...

I'm not afraid of the house.
I'm afraid of the girl holding the key.

Chapter 4

I thought the hard part was getting to Kohl Manor.

I was wrong.

The moment we stepped inside, something shifted.
Time seemed to have stopped.
My heartbeat echoed from somewhere far away —
like I was hearing myself from the bottom of a well.

The walls were too quiet.
The paintings, watching.

This house remembered us.
Or maybe... it remembered *her*.

I wasn't sure which scared me more.

Zara stepped inside and didn't look back.
But I did.

And what I saw chilled me to the bone.

The forest we'd just walked through... gone.
The gate tangled in vines... vanished.
The path that led us here?

Erased — like we were never meant to leave.

A dense fog crept toward the house, thick and fast, like it meant to trap us inside.

I panicked and slammed the door shut, chest heaving.

But when I turned around, Zara hadn't even noticed.

It was like the girl who walked in with me... was gone.
In her place stood someone older.
Stranger.
Claimed.

She didn't look lost anymore.
She looked *chosen*.

As if the house had whispered her name — and she'd finally whispered back.

She moved through the entrance hall like she belonged to it.
Fingers brushing over the walls, the paintings, the furniture... as if she were waking them up with her touch.

I called out to her, but she was somewhere else entirely.
Entranced.

I told myself she was just tired. Overwhelmed. Curious.

But the truth is — I needed space.

Because the only person I love in this world
suddenly felt like someone I no longer knew.

I left her and wandered through the mansion alone.

Every door I opened felt like it might hold a ghost.
Or worse — a truth I wasn't ready to see.

There were dozens of bedrooms.
Each larger than the last.

But one room — at the very end of the corridor — pulled at me.
Not *called*.
Pulled.

When I entered, the scent of jasmine wrapped around me
like a memory I didn't know I missed.

It calmed me.

I sat down on the edge of the bed, taking a shaky breath,
trying to let myself feel something that wasn't fear.

But unease crawled back into my chest.

I turned towards the window, just in time to see something flicker past.
A shadow?
Or just nerves?

I shook it off and stepped into the bathroom.

Clean. Stocked.
Everything in place — and disturbingly familiar.

Every product smelt of jasmine.
My favourite.

Things I hadn't used in years — all here.
Waiting.

Coincidence?

I wanted to believe that.
But even delusions couldn't comfort me anymore.

I filled the bathtub.
Let the steam rise.
Let the fear melt.

I undressed slowly, eyes scanning the corners of the room.
Then I slipped in.

The heat wrapped around me like a second skin.

For the first time in days, I felt like I could breathe.

It began to rain outside.
Thunder rolled overhead.
Loud. Violent.

Like the storm wanted to remind the house
it wasn't the only one that could roar.

Somewhere between fear and exhaustion, I fell asleep.

—

I woke to darkness.

Thick.
Wrong.

The water... wasn't water anymore.

It was heavy.
Black.
Sticky.

I scrambled up and slipped —
my head crashing against the marble edge of the tub.

Pain exploded in my skull.
Warm blood ran down my face,
into my eyes,
into my mouth.

I could barely see.

Somehow, I grabbed a robe, threw it on,
and stumbled out of the room.

My legs barely held me
as I staggered downstairs, calling for Zara.

And then I saw her.

Sitting at the grand dining table.
A feast laid out before her.

She was laughing.
Drinking wine.
Talking.

But she was alone.

No one sat across from her.

I blinked through the blood in my eyes,
trying to make sense of it.

And then —

I saw *him*.

A man.

Just for a second.
Watching her from the shadows.

He didn't move.
He didn't need to.

He knew I saw him.

I screamed.

She was laughing a second ago. But the moment I screamed, her mask cracked.
And there was my sister again — scared, innocent... or pretending to be.

But my vision spun.
My knees buckled.
The world caved in.

And just before the darkness took me, I heard it —

A voice.

Deep.
Male.
Familiar.

"You made a mistake... Mira"

Chapter 5

The first thing I felt was the cold.
Not the kind that brushes your skin —
the kind that *seeps in*.
That burrows into your bones.
The kind that watches.

I opened my eyes to a place I didn't recognise.
Not the bathroom.
Not the bedroom.
Not the spot I collapsed in.

Something had shifted.

I tried to sit up— but my body wouldn't obey.
No movement. No sound.
Just stillness.

Was this sleep paralysis?
A coma?

Why couldn't I move?

I darted my eyes as far as they would go—
but all I saw was black.
An all-consuming, breathless dark.

I've never feared darkness itself.
It's what *lives* inside it that terrifies me.

And right now—
I feel watched.

Zara still looks like my sister.
But something's... off.
There's a *lag* in her smile.
A shadow behind her eyes.

Like the house has started rewriting her—
one memory at a time.

We haven't been here long.
But time in this place moves differently.
It drips.
Like poison.

Slow. Endless.
And with every drop,
I feel my soul bleeding out of me.

Suddenly— a flash.
Too bright. Too fast.

It scorches through the black, and I wince.

When my vision clears...

I'm on a railway track.
Not beside it.
On it.

Bound.

I try to move,
but I'm shackled.

My wrists. My ankles.
Locked in cold metal.

I thrash— but nothing gives.

A train horn wails in the distance.
Closer.
Louder.

It's coming straight at me.

My breath catches.
I try to scream— nothing.
Not a sound.

I try to cry—
but my tears have dried into dust.

Panic claws through me.

This isn't real.
It *can't* be.

But then I see it—
lying next to me on the tracks.

The manor key.

Glowing faintly.
Like it's been waiting for this exact moment.

Zara is nearby.

I scream for her.
Desperately.

But my voice never leaves my throat—
as if the air itself is silencing me.

This is the most helpless I've ever felt.

The train is close now.
Its lights flashing like eyes.

And then—
I hear it.

The voices.

At first, a whisper.
Then louder.

Hundreds.

Thousands.

All chanting my name.

Mira.
Mira.
Mira.

Like I'm some offering.
Like I'm the ritual they've waited years to complete.

And then—

I see her.

Leela Kapoor.
My mother.

She's standing just beyond the tracks—
gripping Zara by the neck.

Tight.
Cruel.

Like she's holding a toy she's about to break.

In her other hand — a blade.
Long. Silver.
So clean, it reflects the oncoming lights.

"No... no, no, NO! Please! Mum, stop!
Take me instead!
She's just a child! Please!"

I'm screaming.
Begging.

But she doesn't hear me.
Or maybe she does — and doesn't care.

And then —
With one smooth motion,
she slices Zara's throat.

The sound— like ripping silk.
The blood— a spray of red across the dark.

This can't be real. But the blood smells real. Too real.

Zara's eyes lock onto mine.
She tries to speak—
but all that comes out is red.

She falls.

I scream until I think I'll rupture.

But she's already gone.

And my mother?

She turns towards me.
Calm.
Expressionless.

She strolls across the tracks—
no urgency, no fear.

Then kneels beside me.
Lays down.
Presses her body next to mine—
like we're just two sisters
lying under the stars.

She brings the knife to her mouth.
Licks the blood from the blade.
Smiles.

My chest tightens.
My lungs don't work.
I can't move.

I can't scream.
I can't *think*.

And all I can say—
over and over again— is:

**"Please...
please, tell me she's okay.
Tell me this isn't real.
I'll do anything.
Just— give her back.
Leela, please. I'll pay any price!"**

Chapter 6

A sharp sting slices through my skull.
Metal floods my mouth.

The floor beneath me is cold — wet.
Too wet.

I jolt awake.

I'm not on the tracks.
Not at the dining table.
Not beneath a sky roaring with trains
or the weight of my mother's sins.

I'm back.
On the bathroom floor.

Soaked.
Bleeding.
Alone.

The tub behind me is still full —
but the water is dark.

Tainted.

With blood from the wound on my head.

I must've fallen.

No... not fallen.

Dragged under.

Like something dragged me into the nightmare
and then spat me back out.

Hallucination.
Sleep deprivation.

No food. No rest.
Too many days of fear compacted into too few hours.

I grip the robe tighter around me,
fingers trembling.

It wasn't real. But the blood on my skin says otherwise. Maybe I'm the broken
one. Maybe this house doesn't even need to haunt me — maybe my own mind
will do the job for it.

I force myself to stand, legs buckling slightly.
The blood clings to my skin, warm and sticky.

I find a towel and try to clean myself —
but it keeps coming.

My head pulses — my vision blurs.
Every step feels like dragging
the weight of my entire past behind me.

I'm slipping.
Even when I hold on —
it's like grabbing smoke.

Reality blurs.
Edges tilt.

And Zara...

Zara is gone.

I spin around.
Call her name.

Nothing.

No sound.
Just the endless stillness of this house.

Did Leela take her?

The walls feel alive. Breathing. Listening. This house doesn't just hold us — it's recreating us. And if I can feel it, then so can she.

It won't take my thoughts.
It won't take my name.
It won't take *her*.

Not again.

Then—

A gust of wind.
Cold. Violent.
Inside the house.

The windows are shut.
My breath fogs instantly.
The air thickens.

And then —

Click. Click. Click.

Heels.
Sharp. Deliberate.

Echoing down the hall like a countdown.

Someone's walking towards me.
Not just walking—
arriving.

Like a storm dressed in elegance.

I squint, blinking against the dim light.

A figure.
Shadowed.
Still.

My heart clenches.

It's Zara.

But not *my* Zara.

She's draped in a long, black lace ball gown.
Heels that echo like hammers.
Gloves— elbow-length. Black.
A large Victorian hat shadows her face.

In her hand—
a lantern.
Flickering.
Burning.

Like my eyes, watching her like this.

I whisper her name.

Soft. Careful.

Like I might wake something
I'm not ready to meet.

"Zara...? Wh-what are you doing?"

She stops.
Mid-step.

As if her name barely reached her.

I shift forward, my hand sliding off the rail I'd been gripping at the top of the stairs.

And she turns.

My stomach drops.

Red lipstick.
Thick eyeliner.
A mole on her upper lip —
one that's *never* existed before.

A gold nose ring.
A pearl-drop necklace, deep crimson,
resting like a curse against her collarbone.

But that necklace...

There's something *wrong* with it.

I squint.
Try to focus.

There's something moving inside it.
Sloshing.

Like molten lava.
Or—

Before I can even process it —

She **shoves** me.

Hard.

Too hard.

I stumble back —
Trip—
Fall—

Down the stairs.

The world flips.
Ceiling. Wall. Light. Darkness.

And just before I crash,
I see it again.

The necklace.
Glowing.

That red liquid inside it —
not lava.

Blood.

Still warm.
Still *alive.*

THUD.

I land hard.
Pain explodes in my ribs.

The ceiling stares back, cracked and unfamiliar.

Blood trickles across my lips again.
But none of it compares to the ache in my chest.

Because my sister just pushed me.

And for the first time, I couldn't tell if she wanted me dead... or if something else wanted it through her.

Chapter 7

I used to wake up hoping.
Now I just wake up hurting.

My ribs throb with every breath, a reminder of the stairs —
or maybe just another dream the house stitched into me.

Either way, pain greets me before hope ever can.

Zara smiled at me this morning —
but it didn't reach her eyes.
Or maybe they weren't hers anymore.

She *looked* like herself again.
Her clothes. Her face. Her shoes.

The red diamond necklace that once stared into my soul?
Gone.

I wandered into the kitchen,
stomach gnawing at itself after days without real food.

Desperate for something.
Anything.

I opened the fridge.

It was full.
Fruits.
Vegetables.
Bread.

Milk.
Yoghurt.

All fresh.

Someone had been here.
Recently.

The day before we arrived —
maybe even hours before.

I turned—

And Zara was standing inches away.

So close,
it felt like I was breathing for the both of us.

"What are you doing?" I flinched.

"Zara... move back. Please."

She didn't.

She just wrapped her arms around me —
tightly, like she was squeezing the soul out of me.

"Did you know that I love you, Mira?"

One sentence.
That's all she said.

And it was enough to send a cold rush
across my entire body.

It was the first time she'd spoken
since we got here —

and somehow, silence had felt safer.

"I... I love you too, Zara."

**"Can I make you breakfast, dear sister?
It's been so long since we sat down together."**

Before I could respond,
she turned away and started cooking.

Cracking eggs.
Slicing mushrooms.
Crisping the bacon on the stove.

Bacon.

With tomatoes and halloumi on the side.

We're vegetarian.
Always have been.

And one more thing —
Zara doesn't know how to cook.

She once burnt toast in four different ways.

She placed the plate in front of me
and sat with her own.

Then bit into the bacon as if it was the best thing she'd ever tasted.

**"Zara... you know this is meat, right?
When did you start eating this?"**

I paused.
"More importantly... since when do you even know how to cook?"

She froze.
Just for a second.

Like a glitch in a program.

Then —

She smiled.
Too smoothly.

**"Mira, what are you even talking about?
We've had this all our lives.
Bacon and eggs, remember?
Dad made it for us every morning before school."**

My blood ran cold.

Dad?

No.
No, he didn't.

He barely made eye contact with us.
He never entered the kitchen unless it was to yell.

He didn't cook —
he commanded.

And Mum cleaned up after his messes,
sweeping silence under rugs
and bruises behind makeup.

"This isn't right," I whispered.
"Dad never made us breakfast.
He barely even looked at us."

Zara didn't react.

She just kept eating.
Calm. Detached.

As if she remembered a childhood I didn't.
Or wasn't supposed to.

I stood up and gently pushed my plate away.
The scent of the meat turned my stomach.

As I reached for my jacket,
my arm knocked over a photo frame
sitting too close to the edge of the counter.

It crashed.
Sharp.
Final.

I bent down quickly.
Too late.

A shard of glass buried itself
deep into my palm.

I gasped —
the pain sudden and bright.

Blood rushed out fast,
spilling across the shattered frame.

Flooding the photo beneath.

I winced as I crouched,
trying to pick up the pieces —

but the image was already ruined.
Drenched in red.

I held it up to the light,
squinting through the mess.

Trying to see who it was.

But all I could see was crimson.
Crimson — and a smile.

Partially hidden.
Twisted.

Unsettling in a way I couldn't name.

I stared too long.
Because something about it felt *important*.

Familiar.

Like a face I should remember —
But couldn't.

And in that moment, I realized the past I trusted was no longer mine.

Chapter 8

I don't remember when the light faded.

One moment Zara was cooking, the next — the windows were black.

Hours gone.

Swallowed.

I walk outside.

More like run.

I need to feel the grass.
Touch the walls.
Hold something *alive* —
Just to believe I'm still real.
Still *me*.

Because inside this manor,
I feel like something's peeled my skin off
and stitched someone else beneath it.

The moment I step into the open —

A cold breeze slices through me.
Like stepping barefoot into snow.

Freezing.
Paralysing.
Numb.

I look at my hands.
Count my fingers.
My toes.
Touch my face.

Everything's in place.
But nothing feels *mine*.

I look up.

It's supposed to be a full moon tonight.

But the sky is blank.
Black.
Unforgiving.

No stars.
No light.
No moon.

I spin.
Once.
Twice.

Nothing.

And when I try to go back inside —

The door is locked.

Panic ignites in my chest.
I run — barefoot, frantic — circling the mansion,
searching for another entrance.

Each step burns.
As if the ground itself is angry at me.

If I stop, I'll freeze here.
Forever.

So I keep moving.
Keep breathing.
Keep trying to exist.

Then —

A voice.

Faint. Floating.

"She won't let you in anymore..."

It stops me cold.
I freeze mid-step.
I can't go forward.
I can't go back.

A silhouette moves in the distance.
Gliding, not walking.

As it nears,
I see it's holding something.
A piece of paper?

I'm hypnotised.
Rooted.

But before I can make a move—

Something grabs me.

Yanks me hard.

And suddenly—

I'm back inside.

Kneeling on the cold floor.
Still holding the shattered glass.
Blood dripping from my palm.

The photo.

I look again.

The image beneath the blood isn't what I remembered.

No girl.
No smile.
No warmth.

Just a night sky.
Empty.
Moonless.

And beneath it —
a silhouette.

Standing in the snow.
Burnt edges.
Frostbitten sky.

Something impossibly *wrong* about it.

But I was just there.
Outside.
Wasn't I?

I look down at my feet.

Cold as ice.
Wet.
Stained red.

The same red as the glowing liquid
in Zara's necklace.

The exact hue of something ancient.
I stumble backwards, knocking over a chair.

The silence that follows isn't empty —
it's *thick.*

Listening.

I glance back at the photo.

The silhouette...

It's not still anymore.

It's moved.
Just slightly.

But enough to be *certain*.

It's watching me now.

I blink.
Once.
Twice.

It doesn't move again.
But I know what I saw.

I wipe more blood off the glass.

There — at the bottom.
Tiny script.
Almost invisible.

"This isn't the first time."

The words punch the air out of my lungs.

I turn.
Expecting to see Zara.
Expecting to see *anything*
but more emptiness.

But I'm alone.

Except I'm not.

Because now I hear it —

Humming.

Soft.
Delicate.

A lullaby I've never heard before.
But somehow...
I know it's meant for *me*.

And one thing I know for sure:

Zara doesn't sing.

Chapter 9

This time — I don't go looking.
I just crawl into bed.
Light every candle in the room.
Lie down.
Tell myself I'll sleep.

But I can't.

All my memories with Zara seem to be fading away.

The girl living with me looks like her — but she isn't warm anymore.

I want to reach out to her and ask her, *where did I go wrong if I just wanted to save her?*

I don't want to say it out loud or even admit it in all honesty.

But she is starting to terrify me.

The way she moves, the way she keeps talking to someone but no one is there?

And why is baba making breakfast in her memory but beating and ignoring us in mine?

How is it that we both have different memories?

She wouldn't lie to me, she is my everything.

So, that means I am missing something?

How is that possible?

The moment I try to sleep —

Something pokes me.
Sharp. Cold. Deliberate.

I sit up, heart already racing.
Reach under the pillow.

There it is.
A folded note.
Tucked inside the pillowcase.

The paper is thin.
Edges torn.

The handwriting — *familiar*.

Like something I saw once —
In a fever dream.
In *his* hand.

You saw me. You just don't know it yet.
Come to the chapel at 2AM.
The truth won't wait forever.

My mind flashes back.
To the silhouette in the snow.
To the shadow holding something.

I never saw his face.
But my body remembers
what my mind can't.

And just like that —
Sleep is no longer an option.

I lie awake, watching the clock.
1:50 AM.

My legs move
before my brain catches up.

I sneak out of the room.

Zara's sleeping —
or pretending to.

Either way,
I don't trust my eyes anymore.

I slip down the hallway.

The air feels... still.
Too still.

Outside, a faint white glow pulses in the distance.

The chapel.

It looks like the moon
is trapped behind its cross.

I follow.
My feet barely touch the ground.
Like something else
is walking me there.

The chapel looms ahead —
Crumbling.
Forgotten.
Cold.

And yet...

Inside,
it feels alive.

Cobwebs drape the pews like funeral veils.
Candles long dead are still stuck to the walls —
as if waiting to be relit by a memory.

No one's been here in years.
But something remembers.

I step forward.
Fingers brush one of the pews.

Dust.
Real.
Physical.

Proof I haven't gone completely mad.
Yet.

Then I smell it.
Jasmine.
Faint but sharp.

And it's coming from behind the altar.

I hesitate.
Then step closer.

FLASH.

A burst of blue light
slams into my vision.

Blinding.
Electric.

I shield my eyes,
pulse thundering in my throat.

But what frightens me the most?
The line between reality and fantasy is blurring way too quickly for my comfort.

The glow.

The silence.

The forest.

The two of us —
Zara and me —
Somewhere we shouldn't have been.

But why does it feel like I've stood here before?"

My eyes adjust — just enough.

And now,
someone stands beneath the crucifix.

A man.
Still.
Watching.

Too still to be human.

My voice cracks.

"W—who are you...?"

He doesn't answer.
Just tilts his head.

Like he's remembering me —
or waiting for me to remember *him*.

The silence stretches —

And then, he finally speaks.

His voice is low.
Dusty.
Like it travelled through time.

**"You always come back here, Mira.
Even when you swear you won't."**

He steps forward.
Half in shadow.
Half in something *darker*.

**"You somehow always make the wrong decisions... How is it that you
always select what is destined to doom you?"**

His eyes find mine.

And I swear —
I've seen those eyes before.

Maybe not in this life.
But *somewhere*.

Some version of me has stood here.
With *him*.

**"This isn't your first 2AM, Mira.
But it might be your last."**

Chapter 10

The glow hit me first— sharp, blinding, too blue to belong to anything human.

His eyes.

Watching me like they'd been here forever.

I should be afraid.

But fear feels dull now.

He says my name like it's his to keep.

Like I've said it to him before.
Impossible.

Leela and Baba barely let me breathe outside our walls.
And yet... he looks at me as though I've been here a thousand times.

I reach for his face.
He steps back.

Controlled.

Almost... rehearsed.

"You don't have much time, Mira. You never do. And yet—" his voice sharpens, "—you waste it."

Before I can reply, he presses something into my palm.
A folded piece of paper.

Our hands brush.
Warmth.
Real warmth — not illusion, not fear.
My chest aches with the memory of warmth.
He's real. He has to be.

I try to read, but his voice cuts in, low and deliberate:
"Not here. Not now. In your room. Alone. And, Mira—"
He leans closer, his breath ghosting my skin.
"Don't let Zara see it. Not her. Not anyone."

The weight of his stare pins me.
I nod. And run.

The night claws at me. The wind shrieks, desperate to rip the note from my hand.
Through the kitchen window, I see her.

Zara.
The necklace glowing red against her throat, pulsing like it knows I'm watching.
I freeze. My lungs forget air.
Then I slip inside — silent, slow.

But just before I reach my room, another door creaks open.
I glance in.

Zara.
Asleep.
Curled beneath a blanket, chest rising steady.

Two Zaras.
One in the kitchen.
One in bed.

My knees nearly give in.
I don't check again. I don't dare.
I bolt into my room. Lock the door. Lock everything.

Every candle I can find — lit.
Every corner — glowing with fragile defiance.

Then, finally, the note.

The paper is damp.
I unfold it with shaking hands.

"She is not where you left her.
You are not who you think.
The house remembers.
The blood repeats.
The cross was never clean.
The snow still holds your name.
When the clock stalls, the truth breathes."

The words bite into me. Too precise to be nonsense. Too heavy to be chance.

Heat blooms under my fingers. The edges curl.
Before I can read it again —

Flame.
Sudden. Absolute.
The page crumbles to ash.

Smoke coils around me.
And I am left with nothing but its whisper.

Zara isn't Zara.
And maybe I'm not Mira either.

Chapter 11

Sometimes, when you try to think too hard, your mind doesn't sharpen — it
shuts down.
It blanks.
You can't process what's right in front of you.

That's where I've been stuck for the past few days.

Trying to connect dots that keep disappearing.
Trying to make sense of the senseless.
But everything collapses before it can form a complete thought.
Everything *fails*.

And now, I don't know what any of it means anymore.

How can a piece of paper — something that was just in my hand — with words
burned into my memory, suddenly ignite and vanish?

When you touch fire, it burns you.

But my hand?

No cuts.
No burns.
No ash.
Nothing.

As if that paper never existed.

But I remember.
I remember every word.

"She is not where you left her…"

And then there's Zara.

I saw her in the kitchen.
That *red glow*. The same dress. The same stillness.
But then — I saw her again.
Asleep in bed.

Which one was real?

Was *any* of it?

I close my eyes, trying to breathe through the pressure building in my chest.
But everything feels tight.
Distant.

My ears ring. Not loud — just enough to push everything else away.
Like I'm stuck *between* two places.
Two *selves*.

Two versions of the same reality — overlapping, just slightly… but wrong.
And I can't tell which one is mine.

I curl up on the bed, tears slipping out without permission.

What have you done, Mira?

Coming to this place… was the biggest mistake of my life.

I should've stayed.
Should've compromised.
Should've endured just a little longer.

Maybe then…
Zara would still be Zara.
And I would still be me.

The regret floods in. Drowns me.

And then —
My body reacts.

My eyes roll back.

Not gently.

Not naturally.

Forcefully.

A vision.

Baba.

Standing in a dark room I don't recognise — but behind him, a golden circle pulses.
Not light.
Something *alive*.
Breathing. Watching.

A girl kneels inside the circle.

I can't see her face —
but I feel her fear like a scream in my own throat.

And Baba?
He just stands there.
Silent. Still.

What even is this?

I'm yanked out of the trance so violently, my body jerks like I've been shocked.
Blood leaks from my nose.
My hands tremble as I wipe it away.

And that's when I realise—

Ever since we came here...
my body hasn't been mine.

Wounds with no origin.
Burns with no pain.
Bruises from nowhere.
Cuts that appear like whispers from another life.

I stumble to the bathroom, desperate to rinse this off — to find something solid again.

I strip off my robe.

And freeze.

Three red scars slash across my stomach.

Perfect.

Parallel.

Precise.

Not scratches.
Not accidents.

Symbols.

They weren't there before.

I didn't fall. I didn't get hurt.

But they're *there*.

And when I run my fingers over them — they don't sting.
They burn.

From *within*.

My heart hammers.
My pulse skids.
My throat dries.

Then—
dripping.

Steady.
Measured.
Like a faucet left on in a silent house.

But I haven't turned on the shower yet.

I turn slowly.

The sound is coming from the bathtub.

Steam curls out from beneath the curtain.
The mirror fogs — but not from me.

My reflection is gone.

Instead— a girl.

Soaked.
Hair clinging to her face.
Eyes locked onto mine.

Wide.
Unblinking.
Wrong.

I can't move.

Because she isn't me but she looks awfully like me.

She raises her hand.

Slowly.

Three fingers.

Matching the scars.

And then she *smiles*.

Not kind.
Not cruel.

Something I can't quite put my finger on.

The fog vanishes.

And she's gone.

Just like that.

I stumble backward, crashing into the bathroom door.

My breath catches in my chest.
Sweat clings to my spine.
My skin prickles like it's being watched.

I glance back at the mirror — praying it stays empty.

And it does.

But there's something new.

A crack.

Thin.

Sharp.

Crawling downward inch by inch.

Alive.

Watching me as much as I was watching it.

Then —
a knock.

At my bedroom door.

Once.

Twice.

And then—

A whisper.
Right through the keyhole:

"I saw you."

Chapter 12

This time, something snaps in me.
I'm done being the frightened, trembling girl they think they can control.
I didn't come here to break.
I came here to survive.
And I won't be bent by things that aren't even human.

"If you want to fight," I shout into the silence, "then have the courage to face me! I'm done hiding. I'm right here — and you know you need me. I don't need you. So do your worst... and I'll watch you fail."

The words leave my mouth like fire — burning away whatever fear I had left.

I step into the shower, cold water crashing over me. Cooling the rage. A fragile truce.
When I glance at the mirror — I see it.

A message. Scrawled in red.
Too bright. Too raw.

*"Don't be so confident, darling.
We might not be so generous next time."*

Blood? My blood?
I smear it with my finger. Metallic. Fresh.
I wipe it away.
And smile.
Let them know I'm not scared anymore.

I storm to the room where Zara slept.
"Zara... can I talk to you?" My voice low. Steady.

No response.
I shake her shoulder. Nothing.
So I slap her— hard.

She jolts upright, gasping. "What the hell, Mira?!"
"Learn to respond the first time. Where did you get that red necklace?"

Her eyes widen, confused. Or just for show.
"I-I don't know what you're talking about... what necklace?"

"Don't lie. You were wearing it. Tell me where it is."

She shrinks against the headboard, voice trembling. "Fuck off, Mira! You're losing it. Get out of my room."
She hesitates. Then— colder. Sharper.
"And don't you dare lay your hands on me again.
I won't be so generous next time."

The words hit me like ice.
The exact phrase from the mirror.

"...Zara," I whisper. "Were you in my room?"

Her voice rises. Desperate. "No! I was sleeping! I'm not up chasing ghosts and hallucinations!"

But I'm not listening.
I'm watching.

Her mouth. Her eyes.
That flicker — just for a second.
Like something wearing her skin slipped.

She doesn't blink.
Doesn't breathe.

"Mira," she says, softer now. Too soft. Sweet like poison.
"Why are you scared of your own blood?"

My veins freeze.
Because I never spoke about the blood.
Never said a word.

But she knows.

She knows.
Because she was there.

Chapter 13

Have you ever watched the most beautiful chandelier fall?
Watched it shatter into a thousand pieces right in front of your eyes?
That's what it feels like right now.
Something precious. Familiar. Safe.
Destroyed.

My body feels hollow.
Unnatural.
Like Zara's been hiding behind a mask... and in one brief slip, I saw the thing beneath.

I step back slowly, not breaking eye contact.
She tilts her head.
Her expression shifts again — soft now. Concerned. Even scared.
But it feels... practiced.

"Mira... did I do something wrong? I'm so sorry! I've been feeling so strange since we got here. Do you feel the same?"

"What did you say to me just now?"
My voice is sharper than I expect. It cuts.

Zara blinks. Innocent. Too innocent.
"Just now? I didn't say anything..."

But I heard her. That voice. Those words.
Etched into my brain like wounds.
And now? She's pretending it didn't happen.
Or worse — maybe she really doesn't remember.

I turn to leave — but something glints near her bedside.
A locket.
Small. Dusty. Almost hidden.
It looks out of place here — like something forgotten, or deliberately tucked away.

Why would Zara hide it?

I need to distract her.
"Actually... Zara, I'm feeling a bit peckish. Would you mind grabbing me something from the kitchen?"

She beams.
Too quickly.
Too wide.

"Of course, my darling sister," she says, syrup-sweet. "I'll be right back."

As she brushes past me, her fingers graze across my stomach— right over the three scars.
She shouldn't even know they're there.
But she touched them like she put them there.

My breath catches.
She doesn't look back.
She just walks away.

I wait a beat — then snatch the locket and slide it into my pocket.
My heart pounds like I've stolen something the house was guarding.

Back in my room, I lock the door.
The balcony.
The bathroom.
I even check under the bed — not because I believe in monsters anymore, but because I've learned that the worst ones don't live under beds.
They live in mirrors.
And they know your name.

The locket lies heavy in my palm.
Colder than it should be.
Colder than anything in this house has the right to be.

At first glance, it's nothing.
Worn edges. Scratched surface. Cheap. Forgettable.

But then I see it — engraved faintly on the back:
R.A.
Rudraansh Awasthi.

The name slices through me like a knife dipped in memory.
I haven't thought about him in years.
Not since those strange winter nights. When the lights flickered. When Zara
always got sick.
Rudraansh was there.
Always.
Quiet. Polite.
Watching.
Present in every photo.
Every family dinner.
Every shadow.

Why the hell does Zara have his locket?

My fingers hesitate.
Then slowly — I pry it open.

Inside: a black-and-white photo.
Blurry. Faded. Warped with age.
But I know that face.

Mine.
Younger. Laughing.

And beside me— a boy.
Eyes faintly glowing in the photo's grain.
So faint you could miss it.
Unless you've seen them in real life.

I drop the locket.
It hits the floor with a metallic ting — but the sound doesn't stop.

It stretches, deepens, as if the house itself is chewing on it.

I turn to the mirror.
Just me.

Until it isn't.

Another me.
Behind me.

Her reflection smiles.
Too wide. Too knowing.

Her lips move.
No sound.

The lights flicker.
And her whisper slithers through the room:

"You shouldn't have taken it."

The lights burst.
Glass explodes.
And I fall backward — into darkness.

Chapter 14

Darkness.

Not just the absence of light — but a swallowing black. Thick enough to choke on.

For a moment, I don't know if I'm awake or unconscious.

The only thing anchoring me to reality is the sound of my breath — ragged, uneven, panicked.

I force myself upright.

The mirror is ruined.

But the message?

Gone.

No red letters. No warnings.

Just cracks. And my reflection — splintered, fractured, almost unrecognisable.

I crawl towards the floor, reaching for the locket.

It hasn't moved.

As if even gravity refuses to touch it again.

This time, it's warm in my hand.

Pulsing.

Alive.

The photograph is gone.

In its place: a tiny scrap of paper.

Scrawled in crimson ink — one word:

"Basement."

I freeze.

We don't have a basement... *do we?*

But then — like a hand pulling back a veil — I remember one.

A stone stairwell.

A rusted iron door.

A type of smell I never understood as a child.

Was it always there?

Or has it just... *revealed* itself?

Either way, something isn't just calling me.

It's pulling me.

I tuck the locket away, while the note still burning in my thoughts.

Then I leave my room.

Barefoot. Bleeding. Shaking.

But I don't stop.

Not this time.

I open the door — and she's there.

Zara.

Ear pressed to the wood like she's listening.

She jolts upright the second she sees me.

"What's your problem, Zara?"

Her eyes widen, darting nervously down the corridor.

"I—I brought you something to eat... you said you felt peckish. I knocked, but you didn't answer. I just... wanted to make sure you were okay."

Her voice is trembling.

But the more she speaks, the faker she seems.

My gaze sharpens.

"What did you bring?"

She hesitates. "Just... toast and jam."

Toast and jam.

Something I never really enjoyed eating in all honesty.

My Zara knows that.

I look down at the tray in her hands.

There's no jam.

Just something red.

Smeared across the toast like it was done in a rush.

Or by someone who doesn't know what jam is supposed to look like.

It looks very similar to something I don't want to think about.

My stomach turns.

"I'm not hungry anymore," I say flatly, stepping past her.

Her eyes follow me.

Unblinking.

That smile— too wide.

Too wrong.

As I round the corner, I hear it.

A whisper.

Almost too soft to catch:

"The basement remembers you, too."

I stop.

Not because of *what* she said.

But because she shouldn't know.

I didn't read the note aloud.

I didn't *react.*

How the hell did she know?

I don't turn around.

I just keep walking.

Faster now.

The halls stretch. Thicken. Breathing me in like lungs that aren't mine.

I pass the old grandfather clock on the landing.

Still stuck at **3:12.**

Has it moved at all since we got here?

I press my palm to the wall beneath the staircase — the one I've passed dozens of times.

This time, it gives in.

Like it was *never solid* to begin with.

Click.

A seam splits open.

A narrow wooden door groans forward — hinges moaning like they've been holding in a secret too long.

Behind it: **stairs.**

Stone. Dust-covered.

Leading into a black that feels older than the house itself.

I stare down at it.

And something stares back.

Not fear.

Not even curiosity.

Just **inevitability.**

I place my foot on the first step—

Creak.

A floorboard behind me.

I turn around.

Zara.

Standing still in the hallway.

Face half-hidden in shadow.

"Did you say something?" I ask.

She doesn't respond.

But there's a smile forming.

And then —

The door creaks wider behind me.

Like it's been expecting me all along.

Like it remembers me better than I remember myself.

Chapter 15

I enter the basement.

Slow.

Steady.

Alert.

There is no light in here, so I have to trust my instinct.

Every step echoes. The silence is so deep, it roars.

It's like playing Hot and Cold.

A game Zara and I used to play when we were little.

When you got closer to the object, she'd yell, *"Hot!"*

And when you wandered too far— *"Cold!"*

Sometimes she'd laugh and say, *"You're frozen, sissy! How does your gut always betray you?"*

We'd laugh for hours. Hide sweets in the weirdest places.

The attic. The folds of Leela's shawls. Once— inside an old chandelier.

Those memories feel like another lifetime now.

Everything was easier then.

Kinder.

I miss her.

So much that I don't even know how I'm still standing.

She's not my little baby anymore.

She doesn't laugh like that.

Doesn't *look* at me like that.

Now when she looks at me... it's like she's seeing through me. Or past me.

But right now, I can't afford to think about that.

I can't afford to cry.

I need to survive.

I walk deeper into the room. Each step feels like my shoulders are getting heavier with burdens I am too young to carry.

And then—

The lights burst on.

Too bright. Blinding.

My eyes water. It takes everything in me not to scream.

I squint as my vision adjusts.

This room... it's clean.

Way too clean.

No dust. No cobwebs. No sign that this place has been untouched.

Someone's been here.

While I was upstairs— pretending to sleep, escaping my thoughts.

How did I not hear anything?

Then I see it.

A cupboard.

Massive. Floor to ceiling.

Too big to be here. Too heavy to have been brought down quietly— or alone.

It would've taken four people to carry it at least.

My breath catches as I move closer.

It's hand-painted.

Not just decorated — *crafted.*

Moons. Suns. Celestial symbols. Zodiac constellations. Ancient texts in a language I don't recognize.

There's something hauntingly beautiful about it.

It's the first thing in this house that brings me the slightest sliver of peace.

Until I spot it.

An engraving on the side.

Faint but deliberate.

R.A.

I reach out and trace the letters.

And the cupboard groans.

It begins to open.

I step back, heart pounding in my throat.

But before it does, a thought claws at me:
It's too deliberate. Too neat. Someone wants me to remember him.

Inside— hangs a dress.

A wedding dress.

Red and gold. Traditional. Regal.

But soaked.

Drenched in something deep and dark.

I don't want to touch it.

I shouldn't.

But my hand moves on its own.

As soon as my fingers brush the fabric—

My eyes roll back.

A vision slams into me.

A chapel. Silent.

A girl sits on a pew.

Sobbing.

Another stands at the altar.

In that same red and gold dress.

Her veil is torn. Her face—blurred.

Like my mind refuses to see her clearly.

But I feel her pain.

It's crushing. Suffocating.

And then—

I see them.

Three shadows at the back of the chapel.

One lighter than the rest.

Watching.

Still. Silent.

Like statues made of smoke.

One of them steps forward.

He's tall. His face hidden in shadow.

But he wears *that* red necklace.

The one I saw on Zara.

He raises his hand.

And the girl at the altar—

Screams.

My breath tears from my chest as I'm yanked back to the present.

The vision ends.

I collapse against the cupboard.

I'm shaking.

There's an awful taste in my mouth.

My hands won't stop trembling.

Everything hurts.

The air feels like thick oil — sticking to my skin, choking me.

I try to stand.

That's when I see it.

A small velvet box on the floor.

I pick it up.

A ring box.

I open it.

Empty.

Except for a folded piece of paper. Tucked neatly inside.

The same handwriting as the chapel wall.

"We already chose the bride."

The lights flicker.

Once.

Twice.

And then they die out—

But something breathes behind me.

A whisper — directly in my ear:

"Do you remember saying yes?"

I turn around.

But there's nothing.

Just shadows.

And somewhere in them—

a man laughing.

Low. Calm.

Cruel.

Like he's been watching this whole time.

Chapter 16

I don't scream.
Even though my throat begs to.
Even though the laugh— cruel and distant— still lingers in my ears like an echo too stubborn to die.

I just stand there.
Back pressed against the cupboard.
Breath shallow.
Heart pounding like it's trapped in a ribcage too small.

The room stills.
But something in me shifts.

I close the ring box and slide it into my pocket with trembling hands.
A splinter digs into my palm — I don't flinch.
The pain is grounding.
Proof that I'm still here. Still real.
Still not one of them.

Behind me, the cupboard groans again.
I turn — just in time to see a panel shift.

A hidden passage.
Narrow. Carved in stone.
Lined with flickering candlelight.

Of course.
This house isn't done with me yet.

I should go back upstairs.
Tell someone. Wake Zara — if she's even *Zara* anymore.
But I know I won't.

Because I need to know.
I need to understand.
Before this place swallows me whole.

I step inside.

The air grows damp — thick with the scent of wet stone and something older.
Something forgotten.
The deeper I go, the quieter it gets.
Even my heartbeat softens, like it doesn't want to be heard.

The tunnel opens into a small circular chamber.

Stone walls.
Cracks like veins.
Symbols I don't recognise — moons, stars, serpents, sacred geometry inked into
the rock like ancient warnings.

At the centre: a wooden table.

And on it — a folded piece of paper.

My stomach knots.

I step closer.

Same handwriting. Same jagged strokes.
The same hand that wrote the note that burned.

The one he gave me.

The man with the blue eyes.

I stare at the paper.

We are not all your enemies.
Look behind you.

I freeze.

And turn.

He's there.

Not a vision.
Not a flicker in the mirror.

A man.

Tall. Disheveled. Shadowed.
And those eyes — blue.
Not just bright.
Unnatural. Luminous.

The same blue from the chapel.
From the locket.
From the dream that never really felt like a dream.

My heart leaps into my throat.

"You," I whisper.

He steps forward, hands open. Unarmed.
Unthreatening.

"Mira."

He says my name like he's said it a hundred times before.
Like it belongs to him.

I don't move. "You were in the chapel."

He nods.

"You gave me the note."

Another nod.

"You burned it."

A faint smile. "Some things are meant to vanish."

I don't let up. "What do you want from me?"

He watches me for a long moment.
Like he's measuring how much truth I can take.

"I want you to see what's really happening here. Before it's too late."

"That's vague," I snap. "Try harder."

His lips twitch— amused. "Still as sharp as I remember."

The words land like a strike to the gut.

"You say it like we were close," I murmur.

He tilts his head. "Maybe not in the way you think."

He steps into the candlelight — fully.
And I see him.

I remember.

The boy from the locket.
From the Christmases.
The one who never spoke much — but always *watched*.

"You were always at the manor," I say slowly. "Quiet. Following my cousin around."

"You used to hide chocolates under the stairs," he replies. "And blame your sister."

I blink. "How do you remember that?"

His gaze softens. "I remember more than you think."

I want to call him a liar. None of this makes sense.

But something about him feels *familiar*.

Not in the way you remember a face.
In the way your body remembers a feeling — long after your mind has forgotten.

"What are you doing here?"

"I've been trying to reach you," he says. "But this place... it doesn't make that easy. Not for me. Not anymore."

"Why me?"

His expression shifts.
Not cold. But dense.

"Because they've chosen you. And I don't think you understand what that means yet."

I step back — but he doesn't follow.

"I'm not here to hurt you," he says gently.
"In fact, I might be the only one trying *not* to."

"From what?"

He hesitates.

And for the first time — I see it.
Fear.

Not for himself.
For me.

"I can't tell you yet," he says. "But when the signs return— remember this moment, and... remember me."

He pulls something from his coat and places it on the table.

A pendant.

Glass. Red. Fractured.

Not Zara's necklace — older, dimmer, as though it has already endured more than it should.

It feels almost fragile in the way broken things sometimes are— precious, but dangerous to hold.

"For when the dream become too real," he says.

He doesn't step closer.
But warmth floods the air between us.

Something so gentle, so utterly *kind*, it almost hurts.

It wasn't warmth you trusted— it was warmth that crept under your skin before you even noticed.

The kind that makes you feel closer to someone you still know better than to believe.

"Don't trust the silence," he whispers. "It remembers everything."

The candles don't flicker when he leaves.

It's like the shadows swallow him — and I can't tell if he was ever real.

I stay frozen.
Because in this house where mirrors lie,
and blood speaks,
and shadows breathe...

That warmth shouldn't exist.

But it did.

And it left me split in two.

Half of me wanted to trust it—

to believe someone could still be kind here.

The other half knew better.

In this house, nothing comes without a price.

Chapter 17

The walls felt closer this morning.
As if the house had shifted in the night — just enough to notice, not enough to escape.
The pendant Rudraansh gave me lay on my chest, warm and beating... like a second heart.
And when I looked in the mirror, my reflection was still sleeping.

Did I do the right thing by taking this pendant?
I'm not sure.
But with it pressed against my skin, I feel like I belong to something. Or worse — like something belongs to me.

Zara walked in without knocking.
I flinched and quickly tucked the pendant beneath my top.
She didn't notice— *I hope.*
She just climbed onto the bed beside me, curling into my side like she used to when we were kids.

My breath hitched.

"Mira... can I tell you something?" Her voice was small. Too careful.

"Yes, Zara. Go on," I said, hesitating before placing a hand on her back. Her body was warm, but something about her touch felt unfamiliar — like hugging a fading memory.

"You don't talk to me anymore. You don't sit with me, you don't... *see* me. I look for you, and it's like you've already vanished before I get there. What happens at night, Mira? Why do you vanish like you never existed at all?"

Her voice cracked on the last word.

And I don't know what scared me more — her sadness, or the possibility that she was right?

I wanted to comfort her. To hold her and promise I'm still the Mira I've always been.
But... what if I'm not?
What if this house has changed something in me that I can't even see?

I stayed quiet. And in that silence, something shifted between us — a thread tightening, trembling, just before it snaps.

Zara pulled away gently and sat up on the bed. "I hear you at night. Whispering. Not to yourself — to *someone*. Last night, I heard a name... Rudraansh."

Her tone wasn't accusatory. Just curious. But I flinched anyway.

She noticed.

"You've been different ever since that first night," she added, her eyes searching mine. "The blood. The hallucinations. The basement. The locket you never showed me."

I opened my mouth — but nothing came out.

Then she did something I wasn't prepared for.

She reached across to the nightstand drawer and pulled out a journal.

"You were writing in this yesterday," she said, flipping to a page marked with a loose petal from a dried rose. "You underlined this part like it meant something."

I frowned.

She handed me the page.

It was my handwriting.
My pen.
My voice etched into the lines.
But I had no memory of writing it.

The passage was underlined twice in deep black ink:
"Her smile is trying too hard to be human."

Zara stared at the words longer than I did.

Her thumb grazed the ink, slow, uneasy.

"That doesn't sound like something you'd write for yourself," she whispered. "It sounds like... like you were trying to remind yourself of something. Or someone."

My blood ran cold. I would've remembered writing something like that.

It wasn't poetic.

It was a warning.

My hands trembled as I closed the book. "I didn't write this," I whispered, but I didn't believe my own words.

Zara didn't press. She just watched me — her expression unreadable.

"I'm worried about you," she said. "You're seeing things that aren't there. Or maybe they are, and I just can't see them. But you... you're not all here, Mira. Not anymore."

I stood up too fast. My vision tilted. "You think I'm crazy?"

"I think something is happening to you," she replied, her voice calm. "And I think this house is making you forget which part of it you came from."

That stopped me.

She looked down at her lap, fingers curling into the edge of the comforter. "Sometimes I wonder if the real you ever came inside at all..."

I opened my mouth to respond — to defend myself, to insist I was still me.

But instead, a suffocating terror settled over me.

Because for the first time, I felt it clearly —

my identity flickering like a dying candle, about to be swallowed by something darker.

Chapter 18

I decided to read through the journal that Zara pulled out from my drawer earlier.

Flipping through pages.

Trying to understand who this Mira is that I don't know of — or maybe I don't remember her.

Every page has a drawing in it.

Some scribbles.

Some art.

Some symbols.

And none of it makes sense to me.

One page is torn, violently so, like something was written there and then ripped away in anger or panic.

Then I see it. A single sentence, repeated again and again in my handwriting: **"Don't follow her at 3:12."**

Underlined. Bold. Scrawled in red ink that looks smudged, like someone tried to wipe it off — or cried while writing it.

The time again.

3:12.

The clock outside my room. Stuck there since the first night.

But who am I not supposed to follow?

Another page: two girls.

One labeled "Z."

The other... not labeled at all. Her eyes scribbled out with such rage the paper is ripped through.

It feels less like art and more like a warning.

The handwriting is mine. The memories aren't.

I slam the journal shut, chest rising and falling too fast. Then notice something tucked between the pages — a pressed flower. Jasmine. My favorite.
I didn't put this here. I know I didn't. And yet it smells like it was placed only hours ago.

The shadows in the room lean closer. The air thickens.

"Mira."
Zara's voice from outside my door.

I nearly jump out of my skin. She knocks twice — not loud, not soft, just... careful.

"Mira, can I come in?"

I hide the journal under my mattress.
"Just a second," I say, wiping sweat from my forehead.

When I open the door, Zara's holding a small black notebook.
Not mine. Not hers either.

"I found this in the attic. It had your name on the inside."

Inside the cover: *If found, return to Mira Kapoor.*
My handwriting again. But I've never seen this notebook in my life.

The first page makes my pulse stutter:
"You've already lived through this. You just forgot to remember."

It feels like standing on the edge of a cliff — one breath away from falling apart.

"Zara, can you show me where exactly you found this?"

She nods, carefully, and holds out her hand.
Something about the gesture feels... off. Familiar. But not comforting.
Still, I take it.

We walk, fingers interlocked, toward the attic.
I glance at the hallway clock.

3:12. Again.
Frozen. Always 3:12.

The second I see it, Zara's grip tightens — sharp, sudden, a vice around my wrist.
"Zara, you're hurting me," I wince.

She doesn't respond.
Her fingers dig in harder, cutting off my circulation.

"You're hurting me!" I scream.
But my voice sounds muffled, swallowed by the walls.

And then— the journal's warning flashes in my head.
Don't follow her at 3:12.

I twist, forcing her to face me.

What I see will never leave me.
Her face is gone.
Not wounded. Not disguised. Gone.
Smooth skin stretches where her features should be — no eyes, no mouth, no nose.
As if the house erased her and left nothing behind.

My body doesn't fight. Doesn't flee.
It just... follows. Like this was always where I was meant to end up.

We stop in front of the attic.
The light flickers once— then dies completely.

Only the glow of my pendant remains, pulsing faintly against my chest like a countdown I never started.

The clock at the end of the hall.
Still frozen at 3:12.
But the second hand is moving.
Not ticking. Rewinding.

The journal in my hand grows heavier.
I open it.

The last page has changed.
It wasn't blank before. I know it wasn't.

Now it reads:
"She never dragged you here.
You did.
Check the attic for what you buried."

The attic door creaks open on its own.
And the house exhales — a breath older than me, older than Zara, older than this place.
Waiting.

Chapter 19

The attic door was already open.
Not wide — just enough to let something in.
Or something out.

My hand gripped the edge of the frame.
Colder than bone.
I should've turned back.
But the silence behind me... felt worse.

So I stepped inside.
One foot. Then the other.
The floor creaked under my weight — like it was testing how far I'd fall this time.

The darkness wasn't empty.
It was waiting.

If Zara found something here— I had to find more.
The attic looked centuries old.
Fairy tale furniture. Dustless trunks.
Rows of books stacked like coffins.
Some blank.
Some bled ink when I touched them.
Dates that hadn't happened yet.
Stories that ended before they began.

And then I saw it.
Tucked between two massive encyclopaedias.
A blue book.
Slim. Almost glowing.
It had no dust — as if time hadn't touched it.

I reached for it.
Fingers shaking.
My name was scrawled on the first page—
but not just Mira.
"Property of Mira Awasthi."

That surname.
The same as Rudraansh.

My lungs clenched.

I turned the page—trembling—
and a single drop of ink slid down the corner.

On the second page...
a drawing.
A girl, almost me.
Red wedding dress.
Veil torn.
Face slashed out completely.

And below it, handwriting that wasn't mine:
"The pendant warms you now... but it burned through me."

I stumbled back.
The words seared through my mind.
Burned through me.

Who was me?
And how close was I to her fate?

The pendant pulsed warm against my chest—protective, or threatening. I couldn't tell.

The attic door slammed open.
I whirled around, heart clawing at my ribs.

No one there.
Just the oppressive dark.

When I turned back—
the book was gone.

But the words weren't.
They echoed, unrelenting, inside my skull:
The pendant warms you now... but it burned through me.

And for the first time, a thought broke through my fear:
If I don't find out who she was—
I'll be next.

Chapter 20

Zara was never fond of singing.
She used to say she sounded like a dying whale.
She'd listen to me or Leela hum, but her own voice? She swore it made her skin crawl.

I sat in the kitchen, a full plate in front of me. Untouched. I shifted the food with my fork, pretending appetite.

That's when I heard it.

Humming.
Low. Familiar.

Zara's voice.
Baba's tune.

She used to loathe it — the way he sang it off-key, like a hymn that soured the air. I remembered her exact words:
"Every time he sings, it ruptures my eardrums. If I were him, I'd staple my mouth shut. Save us all the embarrassment."

And now... she was humming it.

"Zara?" My voice cracked.

She blinked, too slow.

"What song is that?"

"What song?" she asked flatly.

"The one you were humming."

"I didn't hum anything. You know I hate singing. Especially not that awful tune
Baba used to hum!" She gave a small laugh and went back to wiping dishes.

I hadn't mentioned Baba. Not his tune. Not his name.
The lie clung to her lips like it didn't belong.

The pendant seared against my chest. Not gently — punishing.
Like it knew I wasn't ready to say the words rising in my throat: *Stop lying.*

So I didn't.
I walked away.

In my room, I froze.

The blue book.
Resting on my pillow.

I hadn't left it there.

I locked the door and picked it up.
The pages whipped open on their own, a storm trapped in paper. They stopped
at a heading scrawled in jagged ink:

Journal Entry 312.

A photo stared up at me.
A family portrait.
Leela. Baba. Rudraansh. Me.
All smiling.

And tucked just behind them — Zara.
Her face had been scratched out. Torn away.

Beneath, furious words slashed across the page:

"She wears your sister's skin, but her voice is not her own."

"Protect her before it finishes what it started with us."

"It will look like Zara. It will sound like Zara. But watch the slips."

"Save her, or you'll lose her — not to death, but to it."

The handwriting was mine. My loops. My strokes.
But it wasn't just me.
It felt layered. A chorus.
Other versions of me, echoing through the book.

My throat tightened.
They weren't condemning Zara.
They were warning me.
Warning me about the thing *inside* her.

I touched the torn edge where her face should have been.
It was warm.
Like someone else had touched it only seconds before me.

And then—

A blinding pull ripped me backward.
The book slipped from my hands.
The room vanished.

Snow.

A hallway stretched ahead — endless, wrong.
Portraits lined the walls, their eyes scratched out, some bleeding down their frames.

At the center —

Zara.
Chained to a rusted iron chair.
Bolted to the ice.

Her lips were cracked. Her breath came in shallow clouds.
She looked up — and our eyes met.

"Didi?" Her voice broke. "Can you see me?"

I stepped forward—

A violent yank tore me back, hooks under my ribs.
The corridor bent, the walls folding inward like paper curling in fire.

Zara screamed.
"That's not me! Don't listen to her — please! I didn't want to leave!"

Her voice echoed.
Twisted.
Then shattered like glass.

The world collapsed.

I slammed back into my body.
Gasping. Choking.

The pendant throbbed against my chest.
I clutched it like it was the only real thing left.

And then—

A whisper slid through the silence.
Low. Velvety. Too close.

"Mira..."

Baba's voice.

The silence after was not empty.
It was waiting.

Chapter 21

His voice still echoed.
Mira...
Velvet-wrapped poison.

I didn't sleep that night.

Instead, I turned to the books.

The first journal Zara had pulled from my drawer was nonsense — broken words, slashed pages, the handwriting mine but the mind behind it alien.
But the blue book—
The moment I touched it, the fog inside me thinned.

The first page: *Mira Awasthi.*
His surname. An uneasy feeling filled me.

The next pages gleamed with golden ink:

Your roses are missing. Think of her, and your heart will lead you toward the truth.

This is your last chance. He is closer than you think.

His soul hides in the amulet. Guard what is left of you.

Not riddles. Warnings.
And the roses—

Zara loved roses. Her soaps, her notebooks, even her band-aids carried that fragrance. Roses were her *mark.*

But here? Since this house? Not once.
Not a single trace.

A memory crashed into me—Zara, chained in the snow. Her lips cracked, her voice weak: *"Didi."*

But the Zara here never called me that. Only *Mira*. Like she knew the name wasn't hers anymore.

I couldn't breathe. I needed answers.

I walked out of my room and started pacing around mindlessly; trying to feel a sense of belonging.

Without realizing, I stood before the basement door.
My hand against the wood.
Cold. Unmoving.

Then—
I hear it faintly.

A sound. Soft. A whimper.

And the air shifted.
Roses.
Thick. Heavy. Flooding me like a memory that knew how desperate I was to believe.

My throat closed.
If it was real—
Could I forgive myself for hesitating?

But if it was bait...

For the first time in years, I prayed. Not to God. Just to *something*.
If she's really there—show me. If not—stop me.

The scent grew thicker, choking the air.

My hand hovered on the handle.
One breath. One twist.

Then—
A voice ripped through me.
Not the door. Not the room.
Inside me.

Hide. From. Her.

The roses soured. Rot crept into their sweetness, and my courage shattered.

My courage broke.
I spun and bolted upstairs, lungs searing, bones shaking.

The kitchen.
Zara stood at the counter.
Her body jittered. Her eyes—brown to grey, grey to brown, glitching like a broken reel.

For a heartbeat—her smirk wasn't hers.
It was Baba's.

"Zara?" My voice cracked.

She stilled. Blinked. Her face softened into calm.
"Tea?" she asked lightly, like nothing had happened.

I stood frozen. My mouth dry.

She went back to straining her tea, that's when she dropped something and then stopped.

She turned around—
Something clenched in her fist.
A sheet of paper.

She stared at me with a level of hate and disbelief I have never seen on her face.

Her hands shook.
And before I could speak—
Her palm whipped across my face.

The slap rang out, loud and final.

"You are a monster!" Her voice quivered with fury. She shoved the paper into my chest. "Was this your plan all along?"

I stumbled back, blinking through the sting. My eyes dropped to the page.

"Dear baba,

I know about your dynamics with Zara and I know if she dies you will be heavily profited because of several things I do not want to get in the details of.

I, as her blood sister and as someone who she trusts blindly is officially ready to support you.

I am ready to kill Zara to earn your trust, in exchange of my freedom.

I will come back home and we can be a happy family again.

I will finish what you couldn't but my freedom should be promised and I will make sure to complete my end of the deal.

Your ONLY daughter (soon),

Mira Kapoor."

I shook my head. "I didn't—"

"Don't you DARE lie to me!" Zara's voice cracked like glass. "This is YOUR handwriting! Your words! He's our father, Mira. Our Baba. Why would he ever want me dead? He loves me. He's always loved me."

My lips trembled. "Zara, listen—"

"No! You listen." Tears welled hot in her eyes. "You've been slipping since we got here. Talking to yourself. Writing things you don't remember. Seeing things no one else sees. And now *this*? I have been there for you, I left home for you, I did everything I could to support you and this is how you repay me?"

Her voice broke into a sob, but her eyes stayed sharp, accusing.
"You're not saving me. You're the reason I might die sooner than I am destined to."

The words gutted me deeper than the slap.
And the worst part?
I am starting to believe her.

Chapter 22

I slammed the door shut behind me.
Locked it. Twice.
My hands wouldn't stop shaking.

Zara's eyes—
No. His eyes. Grey. Just for a second. Just enough.
And the letter... my handwriting. My name. My betrayal.

I clutched the pendant at my neck.
His soul lives in the amulet.
I yanked. It wouldn't come off.

The blue book waited on the bed. My only anchor.
But when I opened it—my words were gone.
Smudged into nothing.
And then, new lines bled across the page in something darker:

Be careful what you believe— lies wear familiar faces.

I dropped it. Stumbled back like the book itself had teeth.
Lightning split the sky. For a second, the mirror lit up—
a silhouette on my balcony. Watching.

I spun. Empty.

And then—
Rudraansh stood at my door.
Calm. Steady. Raindrops clung to his jacket like silver.

"I could tell things were getting worse," he said. "I had to step in."

My throat closed. His eyes swept the room—the scattered book, my trembling hands, the pendant biting into my skin.

"We don't have to talk about it," he added, voice lower. "But I know what it feels like. When the only person you ever loved turns on you."

For a moment, I wasn't insane.
Just... seen.

The storm wailed outside, but he didn't push. Didn't demand.
"I don't need every detail," he said. "But if something's clawing at you... you don't have to carry it alone."

The words cracked something open in me.
The pressure. The grief. The fear.
It all came spilling out—raw and violent—until I sank to the edge of the bed, clutching my knees, gasping through broken sobs.

Rudraansh didn't move closer. Not yet.
He stayed still, watching me unravel.
And maybe that's why—when he finally reached out—I flinched.

"Don't—" My voice cracked.

I didn't trust him.
I didn't trust myself.
Touch meant surrender. And surrender here was death.

But my arms shook. My chest ached. The terror inside me was too heavy, pressing down until it hollowed me out.
And when his hand hovered, patient, steady—
I let it rest on my shoulder.

Warmth.
Solid. Real.
Not forced. Not greedy. Just... there.

I resisted. I swear I did.
But the longer I sat there, the more my body deceived me. Inch by inch, I leaned.
Until the space between us broke, and I folded into him.

His arms wrapped around me. Firm. Unyielding. Like a wall against everything that wanted me broken.
I finally allowed myself to be held.

It wasn't trust.
It wasn't affection.
It was desperation—
a drowning girl clinging to the first thing that kept her afloat.

But the way he held me— steady, unyielding— I couldn't tell if it was for me... or for him.

When I finally pulled back, my face was wet, my throat raw. His hand lingered for a moment, then slipped away. And I hated how much I missed it.

"I don't know if I should trust you," I whispered, breathless. "But I'm so tired of pretending I'm not terrified. Even of myself."

His gaze never wavered.
"I don't expect you to trust me," he said quietly. "But I can stay. For a while. If it helps."

The pendant warmed against my collarbone, pulsing like a second heartbeat.

Comfort was a temporary feeling and peace didn't last.

Rudraansh turned toward the rain-lashed window, his voice a calm warning. "Whatever's pretending to be Zara... it won't hold much longer."

My breath caught.
"What do you mean?"

"They're slipping. Cracking. And when that mask breaks..."
He glanced back at me, steady, unflinching.

"...things get violent."

Chapter 23

There's a part of my memory that feels... wrong.
Not lost.
Tampered.
Like someone rewound it, spliced it apart, stitched the pieces back wrong, and pressed play again.
Now it's clawing its way back.

Fragments.
A corridor that shouldn't exist.
A door that used to be sealed.
The smell of burnt roses drifting from the east wing garden.
The images hit like pulses behind my eyes—uninvited, urgent.
Something is waking up.

Rudraansh is gone.
Vanished the same way he arrived—silent, controlled, a shadow that never belonged to the light.
He left something heavier for me to drown in.

A warning:
"Whatever's pretending to be Zara... it won't hold that form much longer."
The sentence hasn't stopped echoing.
And now the manor feels different.
Denser.
Breathing too close.
As if it heard him too—and hated it.

The blue book trembled in my grip, but for once, it stayed still.
No bleeding ink.
No whispers.

Just silence.
I should've felt relief.

Instead—
CRASH.
Glass shattered.
The window burst inward, shards flying.
A rock skidded across the floor, wrapped in scorched paper.

My fingers shook as I unwrapped it.
The paper was charred, corners curling, still warm.
Seven words:
"Meet me where the roses never bloom."

It hit me like lightning.
I knew exactly where.

When I was six, I'd knelt in the dry dirt behind the east wing.
The part of the garden no one touched.
The soil too sandy, too loose.
Grandpa's voice low beside me:
"No point planting roses here. Too dry. Won't hold the roots. Wind strips the moisture before it sinks."

Back then, it meant nothing.
Now it was a secret someone wanted me to remember.

I stood fast.
Coat. Flashlight.
I was already halfway out the door—

"Going somewhere?"

I froze.
Zara stood at the end of the hallway.
Her posture was stiff, her voice low—too deep, too wrong.

"Going for a stroll?" she asked, one brow raised. "Now?"

My throat dried.
Her eyes were hollow. Empty.

"You've been busy," she said, stepping forward. "Snooping where you don't belong."

Not Zara's phrasing.
Not Zara at all.

"I don't know what you mean," I forced out. "And don't you dare talk to me like that—I'm your sister."

Her smile twisted.
"Of course. Always about respect with you. Always pretending in front of people. But everyone sees you, Mira. Everyone knows what you really are... a sister who plots her own sister's murder."

A migraine throbbed sharp at my temples.
"That's not—"

"You ruin good things. You always do."
She stepped closer. The light caught her eyes.
Grey.

I staggered back.
"You're not her," I whispered.

Her face twitched. Something inside was fighting back.
Then she lunged.

Her hand slammed against my throat, pinning me to the wall.
My head snapped back.
Air ripped out of me.
Her grip was iron.

"You think someone's coming to help you?" she hissed.
"Quit dreaming, darling."

Black ink spilled from the corner of her mouth, dripping to the floorboards.
I clawed at her arms.
She didn't flinch.
My vision darkened.
A high-pitched ringing filled my skull.

My hand flailed—found the vase.
I gripped.
Swung.
SMASH.

She collapsed.
Hit the floor hard.
Still breathing. Out cold.

I didn't wait.
Didn't check.
Didn't breathe.

I ran.
Down the hall.
Down the stairs.
Through the kitchen.
Out into the cold.

The east wing gate loomed—rusted, straining.
I shoved it open.
The flashlight flickered, then steadied.

Dead vines clung to broken trellises.
Soil cracked dry beneath my boots.

And then—crunch.
A photo under my foot.
Faded. Crumpled.
Rudraansh... and someone else, their face blurred out deliberately.
Here.
In this garden.

A whisper cut through the cold.
"You came."

I turned.
Near the splintered trellis—
Still. Pale. Watching.

Leela.

Older. Weathered. Her hair streaked with grey, her clothes too thin for the night air.
Her face carried exhaustion... but her eyes burned with a clarity that unsettled me.

For a heartbeat, relief surged in me.
Family. Someone who might finally understand.

But the way she stood—
Too still.
Too quiet.
As if she'd been waiting for me all along.

My chest tightened.
I wasn't sure if I'd found safety—
Or walked straight into another trap.

Chapter 24

Leela stood still, half-swallowed by the garden's rot and ruin.
For a second, neither of us moved.
The wind bit at my skin, but I barely felt it.

The last time I saw her, bitterness was the only thing we shared.

Now here she was—ghostlike, real.

"Don't come closer," I said.

She raised her hands. Not pleading. Just open.
"I'm not here to hurt you, Mira."

"I don't trust you."

"You shouldn't," she said softly. "But you're in more danger than you think.
And we are running out of time."

Her gaze dropped to my chest.
To the red pendant warm against my collarbone.

Her face changed—terror flickered, then consumed her.
She stumbled back a step, eyes wide.

"Mira," she said, voice strained. "Take it off. Now."

"What? Why?"

She yanked a scrap of paper from her coat, scrawling fast:
Don't speak about it. It hears.

Another line followed:
It's cursed. It's how he's been tracking you.
That thing is listening right now.

My fingers brushed the chain instinctively.
It pulsed.
Not warm. Not cold.
Alive.

Leela scribbled again:
It's not just tracking you. It's anchoring you to him.

I gripped the chain. Yanked.
It didn't budge.
I pulled harder—
Pain lanced across my collarbone.

The pendant tightened like it was part of me.
Refusing to let go.

I cried out.
And then, with one desperate twist—
SNAP.

The chain broke.
The pendant flew to the ground.

HISSSSS.
A shriek erupted from the soil—sharp, piercing, inhuman.
Smoke curled upward as it sank into the dirt.
The ground blackened, sizzling.

Leela stared, frozen.
"Mira," she whispered. "That thing is old. Older than all of us. You never
should've worn it."

We sank onto a crumbling bench. My hands shook.
Leela looked older now—lined, tired.

"What was it?" I asked.

"His mark," she said. "Your father always left something behind to control what he couldn't touch. That pendant—he fed it power. Blood. Voice."

She paused. "The day you and Zara escaped was the last time I ever saw him."

"You mean... he didn't follow us?"

"No. When I went back, he was gone. Not a trace. Which means... he'd already prepared what came next."

Her eyes locked on mine.
"That house wasn't just waiting for you. It was built for you."

A silence pressed in from the trees.
Watching.

"Why us?" I whispered.

"There was someone else," she said. "A black magician. He promised your father legacy. Immortality. But the cost was blood."

My stomach twisted. "Zara and I?"

Leela nodded.
"One of you was meant to die. The other to inherit the power. Balance. One soul to pass. One to receive."

Cold nausea crawled up my throat.
"And then?"

"They would bind you. To him. To... someone else. Someone he promised you to."

"Who?"

"I never saw him clearly. Only his eyes. Blue. Cold. Like the sea at night."

My breath caught.
I thought of Rudraansh.
But said nothing.

"I thought he would've taken you both by now," she whispered. "The fact you're still here means something went wrong."

"I had a vision," I blurted.
Leela's eyes sharpened.
"There's a door. Covered in vines near the garden's edge. I saw it glowing. And Zara—my Zara—was there."

Her lips parted.
"Then that's where we go."

We moved fast, flashlight jerking with each step.
The clearing opened—

And a voice floated toward us.
Soft. Familiar.

"Mama?"

We froze.
Zara stepped out from the trees.
Bleeding. Bruised. Smiling.

Leela gasped.
"Zara..." She ran to her.

Zara's arms opened.
They hugged.

But the hug lasted too long.
Too firm.
Like a man reclaiming what was his.

She whispered into Leela's ear.
And Leela's body stiffened.

She pulled back. Looked into her daughter's eyes.
Grey. Flat. Soulless.

First shock. Then sorrow. Then horror.

"No," she whispered. "Not her..."

Zara tilted her head. Smiled.
"Took you long enough."

Leela staggered back, face crumpling—not with fear, but recognition.
Her hands shook as she looked at me, eyes wide with grief.

She whispered once, then screamed it:

"That's not your sister."
"That's your father."
"He's taken over her."

The air collapsed. My lungs seized.

Zara only smiled.

And Leela—her voice splintered like her soul breaking:
"He didn't just take her. He became her."

Chapter 25

The door was where I'd seen it: vine-choked, half-swallowed by the garden's decay.

Something pulsed behind it. Not light. Not air. **Her.**

I didn't hesitate. I opened it.

Roses hit me the moment I stepped inside—fresh, blooming, unmistakable. A memory made scent.

She stood in the center, barefoot in a white dress that drifted at her ankles. The scar near her collarbone from the bike fall when she was eight. The tilt of her head. Everything right—except the way the air went through her.

"Zara?"

She turned. Her face lit the way only hers could, but her eyes carried a tiredness that hurt to see.

"Didi...?" she whispered.

I reached out. My hand passed through.

"I'm not really here," she said, voice tight. "I'm a fragment. A ghost of myself. I don't know how long I've been like this—or how long I can hold on."

Tears burned.

"I thought I lost you."

"That wasn't me. I've been trying to reach you—dreams, mirrors, the book—but something keeps warping the message. He's stronger now."

"Who?"

She didn't answer. She didn't need to.

"I can't help from here," she said. "I can't hold, touch, warn. I'm barely more than a thought."

"There has to be a way."

"There is. Not alone. You'll need the blade."

"What blade?"

"Bone handle. Old markings. It severs soul-bonds—but only with intention. I don't have it."

"Who does?"

A pause. "I can't say. You'll know it when you see it."

"I'll find it," I said. "I swear."

She smiled, barely. "I've always believed in you."

I forced myself toward the door, then looked back. "I love you, Zara. Your didi's not going anywhere."

"I love you too," she said. "I'll be waiting… till my last breath."

—

The hallway outside felt colder.

"Where were you?"

Rudraansh stood at the far end—still, silent. His eyes swept me with surgical precision and landed on my collarbone.

"You're not wearing it."

I lifted a shoulder. "When I woke up, it was gone."

A flicker—too fast to hold—crossed his face. He didn't press.

"Strange," I said. "You called it protection. You don't seem worried."

"I'm more concerned about you. We don't have much longer left."

"For what?"

"I need you to trust me," he said, softer now. "Everything is accelerating."

He stepped closer. "You once said no one ever really saw you. I did. I do."

"I need you to marry me, Mira."

I frown. "What?"

His eyes glowed faintly blue. "Tomorrow. Before the third hour past midnight. That's when the ritual aligns. It's the only way to protect you."

His smile didn't shift, too smooth, too rehearsed. "The registrar's already prepared," he added, almost casually. "Every union must be written, sealed, witnessed."

"You're scaring me."

"I don't want to. The curse ends tomorrow. I can stop it. But I need you."

His hand lifted toward mine—coat shifting just enough for me to see it: pale ivory, carved with old sigils.

The blade.

Zara's blade.

Pieces locked into place—the book, the pendant, the timing, the blue. Rudraansh Awasthi.

I made myself breathe. Not shake. Not show it.

I let my eyes fill—overwhelmed, grateful, relieved. I stepped into him.

"I... didn't expect this," I whispered. "But I trust you. You've looked out for me."

His fingers tightened around mine. The relief on his face was real.

I pressed to his chest and, in one clean motion, slid the blade from his coat. He didn't notice. The weight disappeared into my pocket like it belonged there.

You thought you could take my sister from me?

Think again, Awasthi.

You don't know who Mira Kapoor becomes when it comes to Zara.

I'll show you what betrayal tastes like.

Wait.
And watch.

Chapter 26

The prayer room was colder than it used to be.
No incense. No chants. Just dust and silence.

Leela stood in the far corner, her fingers brushing an old wooden box — carved and weathered, symbols etched deep like warnings.
She didn't hear me walk in.

"I found this," she murmured, eyes still fixed on it. "It was buried under the floorboard near the altar."
She turned, showing me the hollow groove inside.
Empty. Waiting.

Without a word, I pulled the blade from my coat and slid it in.
It clicked into place like it had never been missing.

The box convulsed.
Blue light burst from the seams—then gold—two forces wrestling for breath.
And then the scream.
Not human. Not animal.
Like something trapped had just been reminded it wasn't dead yet.

Leela stumbled back. "What the hell is that thing?"

"The blade," I whispered. "The only thing that can break what they're trying to do."

And then I told her.
Everything.
Zara. The cursed pendant. The proposal. The truth about Rudraansh.
Every jagged, blood-soaked piece.

Leela's face drained, horror colliding with guilt. Her breath shuddered.
"I should've known," she whispered. "I should've protected you both. I failed you."

Her voice cracked.
And in that moment, she wasn't a mother, wasn't a doctor — just a woman broken by regret.

"I want to help you, Mira. Whatever it takes."

I hesitated. "She needs a body."

Silence.
Then—
"Use mine."

My throat seized. "No. That's not—"

"Yes." Her voice sharpened. "If my body is all I have left to give, then let it mean something. Let me protect her the way I should have from the start."
She took my hands, tight, desperate. "If I die tomorrow, at least I'll die knowing I finally chose my daughters first."

Tears blurred my sight. "Mom..."

But she pressed the box into my palms.
"Call her. Bring her home."

So I did.
Quiet. Intentional.
Zara. We found a way. If you can hear me... it's time.

The air shifted.
The blade hummed.
Leela gasped, knees buckling.
I caught her before she hit the floor.

Her eyes rolled back. Then snapped open.

"Didi...?"

My chest collapsed.
"Zara?"

She blinked—confused, terrified, alive.
"I didn't know if you'd actually be able to do this."

I broke.
I pulled her into my arms, even though the body wasn't hers.

It didn't matter. She was here.

"Zara..." My voice cracked under the weight of it. "That letter—"

Her face softened, just barely.

"I didn't write it," I whispered, the words trembling. "I would rather die a thousand deaths than hurt you. But after everything... after the way you looked at me... it killed me to think you believed it."

For a moment, silence.
And then—her eyes filled, but her voice was steady, certain.

"I know you didn't," she said. "I know it wasn't you. Because nothing in this world, nothing in any world, could ever make you turn against me. Not Baba. Not his curses. Not his lies. They tried to break us, didi, but they'll never win."

Her hand reached for mine, desperate, firm.
"You are my didi. My only didi. If the whole world burns, if we're left with nothing but ashes, I'll still choose you. Always you."

I broke then, truly broke.
Because for the first time since stepping into that house of ghosts, I wasn't just fighting to save her.
She was fighting to save *me* too.

We clung to each other, shaking, crying — until she pulled back, eyes sharp now.

"We need to hurry."

"What happens if the ritual succeeds?"

Her jaw clenched.
"He binds himself to us. Bloodline to bloodline. If it's done, there's no unbinding. Not even with the blade."

"That's why he waits for the eclipse," she said, voice sharp with dread. "When the moon vanishes and the red ring burns, the veil between the living and the dead rips open. At 3:12, the binding can't be undone."

"Then what do we do?"

"We let him believe he's won." Her voice dropped, cold. "But whatever happens—Do not kiss him. Don't let him seal it. Leave the rest to me."

I nodded, still crying, still burning.

"He has the registrar ready."

"Of course he does," she spat. "It has to be official. Sacred. He needs your consent."

"What if I say no?"

Her eyes met mine. Flat. Honest.
"He kills you."

The room fell silent.
Just us, in a borrowed body, with everything to lose.

I looked at the blade glowing faint in the box.
"I'll play along," I whispered. "But the second he looks away..."

Zara nodded once. Fierce. Absolute.

As I turned to leave, her voice stopped me.

"Didi?"

I turned.

Her borrowed face was Leela's, but her eyes were pure Zara.
"I'll be with you. Every second. Until the end."

No tears this time.
Just fire.

She stepped forward, gaze hard.
"He turned me into a ghost."
Her grip tightened on the blade.
"Now let me return the favor."

She glanced at the clock.
"3:12 was the wound he gave us. It'll be the wound that takes him."

Chapter 27

The chapel had never looked more alive—
and yet it was already half-dead.

Flames flickered in the sconces like they knew what was coming.
The velvet drapes hung too still.
The crucifix above the altar tilted sideways, as if turning away from the ritual it was about to witness.

I walked in, wrapped in the blood-soaked lehenga I'd found in the manor's basement closet.
The red had darkened over time, rust-thick, secrets stitched into every pleat.

Zara walked beside me.
Her body was Leela's.
But her soul?
Unmistakably hers.
Her hand brushed mine—a silent vow: *we made it this far.*

At the altar stood Rudraansh.
His smile too wide.
His posture too perfect.
His eyes scanning me like I was both prey and prize.

And beside him—
the registrar.
In Zara's stolen body.
Baba.
Still mocking.
Still hollow.

His grin curled when he saw me, as if this was his wedding gift:
my sister worn like a mask.

"Your sister insisted on attending," Rudraansh said smoothly. "A ceremony like
this—sacred, eternal—felt incomplete without her blessing."

I stayed silent.

Rudraansh reached for my hand.
His fingers locked like manacles.
I let him.

Baba began chanting—verses older than language, heavier than blood.
The blade hidden under Zara's sleeve pulsed once.
Its time was near.

The ancient clock above the altar groaned.
Three deliberate beats.
Tick. Tick. Tick.
3:12.

The veil thinned.
The air itself shuddered.

Rudraansh leaned forward, his breath poison against my lips.
"This is the moment I've waited my whole life for," he whispered.

Inside my head, not aloud, I called to her.
Now.

Zara moved.
Fast. Sharp. Silent.

But Baba noticed.
Of course he did.

He shrieked—
and every candle blew out at once.
The windows shattered.
The mirrors cracked in unison, spilling shadows like blood.
Blue fire roared across the altar.

"WATCH OUT!" Baba thundered.
His voice split the walls.

Zara's body smashed into the pews, skull cracking against wood.
I screamed, lunging for her—
but Rudraansh yanked me back, his grip iron.

"You really thought you could outplay me?" he hissed, voids where his eyes had been. His smile cut like glass.
"You were never a player, Mira. You were the game."

His voice dipped lower, venom thick.
"My grandfather killed yours. All for your father's greed. A legacy bought in blood. I could have freed you. But you wouldn't listen. So I had to hurt you. That pendant you clung to? Mine. It latched your soul to me. Made you feel things that were never real. The scars. The doubt. The need. And that letter?" He laughed, sharp and bitter.
"Your hand moved, but the words were mine. And you believed it. So naïve, my sweet future wife..."

He dragged me toward the altar.
"Do you even remember how many times we've stood here? Five. Five times you tried. Five times you failed. Every death, every drop of blood soaking deeper into the lehenga you're wearing. Do you know why it's so heavy? Because it carries you. Every failure. Every fragile attempt to survive me."

His eyes glowed with fevered hunger.
"This is my last chance. It has to be perfect. Mira, I love you so much it corrodes me. It eats me alive. But if you won't belong to me in life—"
He leaned close, lips grazing my ear.
"—then you'll belong to me in death."

I spat in his face.

"You really thought I didn't notice? That she wasn't my Zara? You stole her soul, wore her like a mask — and you think I'd mistake that for love? You're no savior, Rudraansh. You're just another coward in your cursed bloodline."

His snarl ripped through the chapel.

And that's when she appeared.
Leela.
The real Leela.

Trembling, but her grip steady—
the ancestral blade burning blue in her hand.

Rudraansh's face broke.
"No. Not you—"

"You underestimated every woman in this family," she said, her voice carrying
like judgment.
"First my daughter. Then my silence. Now—me."

She struck.

The blade carved his throat—
and the world cracked open.

Blue fire exploded from the wound, flooding the chapel, searing through his
skin like acid.
Rudraansh screamed—
not human.
Not mortal.
Ancient. Endless.

The chapel shook. Chandeliers burst.
The crucifix fell from the wall.
Outside, the discarded pendant burst into flame, fire rushing inward to devour
the house from its bones.

Baba tried to flee—
but Zara stood in his path.
Back in her own body now.
Whole. Risen.

"No more," she said.

And in her voice was every night of our childhood.
Every laugh. Every promise.

Baba froze.
Because he knew she remembered.

Zara raised her hand.
And he combusted from the inside out.
No scream.
Just bones snapping, smoke curling, silence.

The walls caved.
The roof split.
The chapel collapsed.

We dragged Leela out—her body limp, her pulse faint, her lips murmuring
words we couldn't catch.
The fire chased us, clawing, furious.
We stumbled into the cold night.
Collapsed in the dirt.
Coughing. Crying. Alive.

Zara clutched her own body—scarred, bloodied, but hers again.
I held Leela.

For a moment, everything stilled.
Then—

Leela gasped.
Coughed like a drowning woman breaking the surface at last.

I sobbed into her shoulder.
She touched my face, weak but certain.
"I'm sorry," she whispered. "For everything I couldn't stop. For everything I let
you carry alone."

I shook my head through tears.
"You gave us everything tonight."

Zara knelt beside me, her voice breaking, but strong.
"No letter, no curse, no monster could ever break us apart again. Blood doesn't
bind us. Love does."

And I collapsed against her, all of us tangled in soot and ash—
but together.

Above us, the clouds have calmed down and the eclipse has finally ended.
The moon returned, whole and pure, silver light washing over us.

And after a very long time,
we were free.

Epilogue

One Year Later.
Same night. Different moon.

The living room was warm.
Leela curled on the couch, flipping channels without watching.
Zara sat at the window, sketching — her pencil moving like muscle memory.
I buried myself in a book.

We didn't talk much.
Not because we couldn't.
Because silence was safer.

We'd moved far away.
New names. New walls.
No shadows.
At least, that's what we told ourselves.

Leela stopped on a news channel.
The anchor's voice was flat:
"This is the first lunar event of its kind — a no-moon eclipse with a red corona.
Astronomers say it defies classification. **It began precisely at 3:12 AM, an unprecedented alignment.**"

Zara's hand stilled.
And then—
a drop of blood fell onto her sketch.
Right on the moon.

She stared at it.
Not shocked.

Not scared.
Just breathing faster.

I felt it too.
The weight. The shift.

Leela turned.
Her eyes met mine.

No one spoke.

Because we knew.

The manor burned.
But darkness doesn't die.
It waits.
Like the moon.
And when the night is silent enough—
it returns.

The Silent Eclipse Playlist

Not everything that haunts you comes from memory.
Some echoes slip into songs.
These tracks found me while writing, the way whispers find empty rooms.
If you listen closely, maybe you'll hear what Mira heard too.
Maybe you'll feel it.

— □ —

- **Dark Paradise** – Lana Del Rey

- **Everything I Wanted** – Billie Eilish

- **No Time to Die** – Billie Eilish

- **When the Party's Over** – Billie Eilish

- **Skyfall** – Adele

- **Bury a Friend** – Billie Eilish

- **I Love You** – Billie Eilish

— □ —

(Play them in silence. Play them in shadows. They were never just songs.)

Author's Note

I didn't set out to write a book.
I set out to understand what had been haunting me.
What began as scattered thoughts in the margins slowly grew into Mira. Then Zara. Then a story that refused to stay quiet.

Silent Eclipse is fiction — but it holds truths too heavy to speak plainly.
It's a mirror of things I feared, loved, lost, and survived — reimagined through a darker lens.

This book is not about answers.
It's about questions that twist, linger, and sometimes echo louder in silence.
It's about the weight of memory, the lies we tell ourselves to survive, and the blurred lines between love and manipulation.

If you made it to the end, thank you.
For your time, your trust, and your willingness to be unsettled.
If you felt seen — even for a moment — then this strange little story found the right hands.

I'm honored it was yours.

— *Pooja Rajnani*

Acknowledgements

To my younger self —
You were never too much. You were just ahead of your time.
This book is for the girl who cried herself to sleep, who made homes out of notebooks, and who searched every shadow for something that looked like safety.
You made it here. I'm proud of you.

To my readers —
If this story found you, then maybe it was meant to.
Thank you for holding my words close, for walking through the dark with me, and for letting this strange little book live in your mind, even for a while.

To my sister, Tania —
You are my everything. My why. My home.
Every sentence carries the weight of how much I love you.
You are the calm after every storm and the light I never knew I needed until you arrived.

To the one who helped me hold the pen when my hands shook —
You know who you are.
Thank you for never letting me forget what this story was, even when I did.
For the midnight motivation, the structure when I had none, and the belief when mine ran out.
This wouldn't exist without your voice echoing quietly beside mine.
Even when no one else could see it — *you always knew how the chapter would end.*

And to anyone reading this who feels like their story doesn't matter —
I promise you it does.

Even the broken bits.
Especially the broken bits.

We all carry ghosts.
But some of us turn them into novels.

And if you find yourself looking in the mirror tonight...

look twice.

With all my haunted love,
Pooja Rajnani

www.ingramcontent.com/pod-product-compliance
Lightning Source LLC
Chambersburg PA
CBHW032026180726